Just Me

Story and pictures by MARIE HALL ETS

SCHOLASTIC BOOK SERVICES

NEW YORK · TORONTO · LONDON · AUCKLAND · SYDNEY · TOKYO

For A. H. H.

Copyright © 1965 by Marie Hall Ets. This edition is published by Scholastic Book Services, a division of Scholastic Magazines, Inc., by arrangement with The Viking Press, Inc.

17 16 15 14 13 12 11 10 9 8 7   8 9/7 01/8

                                                                    07

SEE SAW
books

Printed in the U.S.A.

Just Me

A little bird sat on a post by the barn. He was singing with joy to greet the new day. He did not know that Biddy, our cat,

was creeping up through the grass — ready to catch him.

"Fly, little bird!" I called and I clapped. "*Quick!* Fly away!" And

he did. That made Biddy mad, but she walked back through the grass
to hunt something else. And I followed and I walked just like her.

Over by the gate Cocky the rooster was looking for worms.
"Cocky," I said, "I can't fly like a bird, but I can walk like

a cat, and I can walk like a rooster. Let me see how a rooster walks.
So Cocky walked on. And I folded my wings and walked just like him.

Pearl, our pig, was taking a bath-and-nap in some mud. "Pearl," I
said, "let me see how pigs walk." But Pearl was too lazy to get out

of the mud. So I lay down beside her and I took a bath-and-nap too.
(But I took *my* bath-and-nap on dry ground because I had my clothes on.)

A rabbit was nibbling some leaves off a bush. "Rabbit," I said.
(He didn't have any name because nobody owned him.) "Rabbit, I can't

fly like a bird, but I can hop like a rabbit. Let me see how you
do it." So rabbit went off hoppety, hop, hop. And I hopped just like him.

A snake went wriggling through the grass. "Snake," I said, "I can't fly like a bird, but I can wriggle like you. Let me see how you do it."

But 'fraidy-cat snake darted off down his hole so fast that I couldn't even see how he did it. So I'm not sure that I wriggled just like him.

Lulu the cow was out in the pasture eating grass to turn into milk. "Lulu," I said, "I can walk like a cow. Let me see how you do it."

Lulu didn't stop eating, but she took a few steps to show me.
So I put down my head and ate grass, too, and walked just like her.

In front of the barn I met Gongky the goose. "Gongky," I said,
"I can't fly like a bird, but I can walk like a goose. Let me see how

you do it." Gongky spread his wings and started to run. So I spread my wings, too, and I ran just like him.

Old Flora, our horse, stood under a tree. She was thinking of something. I don't know what. "Flora," I said, "I can't fly like a bird,

but I can walk like a horse. Let me see how you do it." So Flora
opened her eyes and walked on a few steps. And I walked just like her.

A squirrel sat under the oak tree. He was biting the shell off a nut. "Squirrel," I said, "I can hop like a rabbit and walk like a horse,

and I think I can climb like you. Let me see how you do it." So
squirrel dropped his nut and climbed up the fence. And I climbed up too.

Spunky the goat was over by the fence eating flowers and weeds.
"Spunky," I said, "let me see how you walk." But Spunky didn't *want*

to walk — she wanted to *butt*. She put down her head and kicked her legs and butted. So I put down my head and I butted just like her.

Over by the haystack I met a frog. He was just keeping cool in the shade. "Frog," I said, "I can't fly like a bird, but I can hop

like a rabbit and climb like a squirrel and leap like a frog. Let me
see how you do it." So frog leaped away. And I leaped just like him.

Down near the woods I met an old turtle. He wasn't doing anything at all. "Turtle," I said, "I want to walk like you. Let me see how you walk."

And I touched him with a stick. But old turtle just pulled in his head and legs and hid in his shell. So I hid in my shell too.

When I came through the cornfield I could see the pond. And there was Dad. He was untying the boat. "Dad!" I called. "Dad! Wait

for me!" But Dad didn't hear. So I started to run. And *now* I ran
like nobody else at all. JUST ME. And when Dad heard me he

waited and helped me into the boat. And together we went to sea,
Dad and me, on the pond at the end of the cornfield.